For Marynell Bryant, a teacher who well understood what I loved —C. B.

For Erin, Nicholas, Megan, and Noel —A. S.

First published in the United States of America in October 2017
by Bloomsbury Children's Books
www.bloomsbury.com

Bloomsbury is a registered trademark of Bloomsbury Publishing Plc

For information about permission to reproduce selections from this book, write to
Permissions, Bloomsbury Children's Books, 1385 Broadway, New York, New York 10018
Bloomsbury books may be purchased for business or promotional use. For information on bulk purchases
please contact Macmillan Corporate and Premium Sales Department at
specialmarkets@macmillan.com

Library of Congress Cataloging-in-Publication Data
Names: Barton, Chris, author. | Spires, Ashley, illustrator.
Title: Book or bell? / by Chris Barton ; illustrated by Ashley Spires.
Description: New York : Bloomsbury, [2017]
Summary: Engrossed in a book, Henry decides to ignore the school bell, which sets off a chain reaction.
Identifiers: LCCN 2017007101
ISBN 978-1-68119-729-6 (hardcover) • ISBN 978-1-68119-714-2 (e-book) • ISBN 978-1-68119-715-9 (e-PDF)
Subjects: | CYAC: Books and reading—Fiction. | Bells—Fiction. | Schools—Fiction. | Humorous stories.
Classification: LCC PZ7.B2849 Boo | DDC [E]—dc23
LC record available at https://lccn.loc.gov/2017007101

Art created with watercolor, ink, and—due to the interference of kitten paws—some digital adjustments
Typeset in Bookeyed Martin, Revivl555, and Zoinks
Book design by John Candell
Printed in China by Leo Paper Products, Heshan, Guangdong
3 5 7 9 10 8 6 4 2

All papers used by Bloomsbury Publishing, Inc., are natural, recyclable products made from wood grown in well-managed forests.
The manufacturing processes conform to the environmental regulations of the country of origin.

Book or Bell?

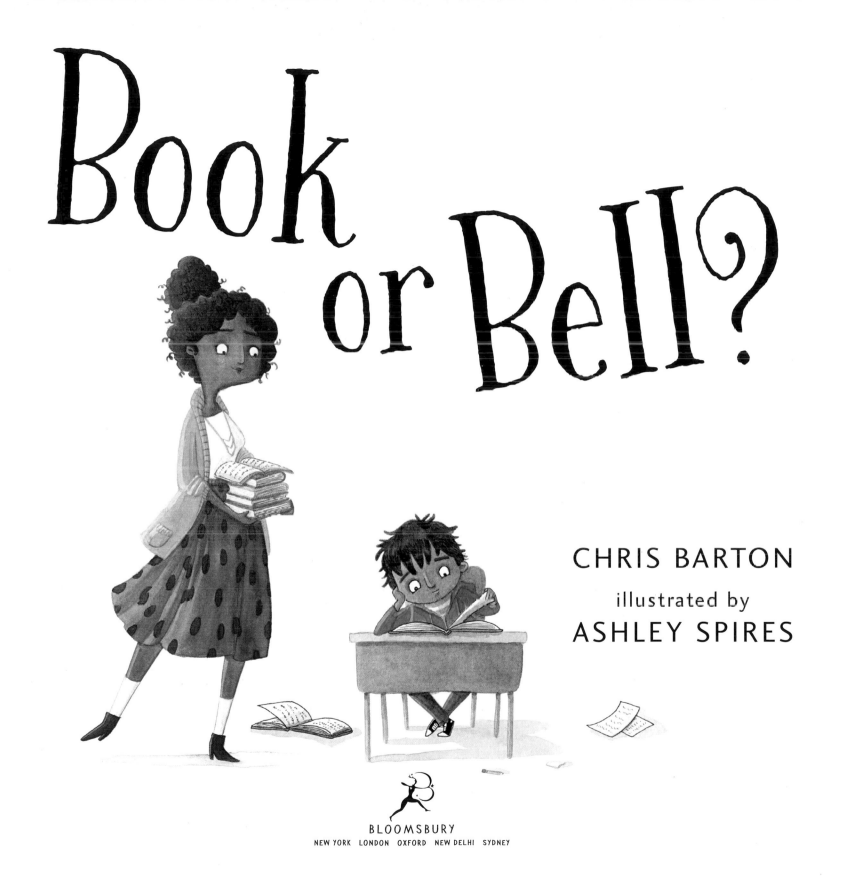

CHRIS BARTON

illustrated by
ASHLEY SPIRES

BLOOMSBURY
NEW YORK LONDON OXFORD NEW DELHI SYDNEY

One Tuesday morning, Henry found the most awesome book about a bike.

The first page had him hooked.

The second page had him captivated.

The third page . . .

BBBBRRRRIIIIIINNNNNGGGGG!

Phooey.

. . . would have to wait.

It was the best book Henry had ever read.

Maybe the best one ever written.

BBBBRRRRIIIIINNNNGGGGG!

Awwwww...

Definitely the best one ever interrupted.

It was incredible.
Amazing.
Simply stupendous.
Who knew?
Whoever would have thought?
Who—

BBBBRRRRIIIIINNNNGGGGG!

Nooooooooo!

—could be bothered by a *bell* at a time like *this*?

Henry had always done what the bell told him. But that was before this day. That was before this book.

Today, instead of going to lunch, Henry decided to just keep doing what he was doing.

He decided to just keep reading.

He decided to just stay put.

The school was not prepared for anyone to just stay put.
By not springing up with the ringing of the bell, Henry set off a
chain reaction unlike anything they'd ever seen.

There was an empty space where Henry's tray would have been.

The food that would have gone on Henry's tray went—
SPLOT!—onto the floor.

The shoe that stepped on Henry's
food went **SCHWOOP!**

"He won't budge," Henry's teacher told the principal. Ms. Sabio was about to explain *why* when—

"I've got it!" interrupted Mayor Wise. "Clearly, you need . . ."

"... a louder bell."

On Wednesday morning, the old bell was replaced
by the latest in nerve-jangling technology.

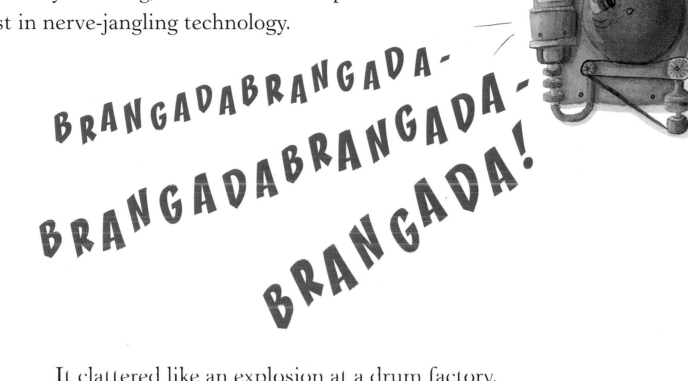

BRANGADABRANGADA-
BRANGADABRANGADA-
BRANGADA-
BRANGADA!

It clattered like an explosion at a drum factory.

The noise made every curly hair straighten. It made every
straight hair stand up. It made every bald head pucker.

But Henry did not stop his reading.
He decided to just stay put.

Without Henry present, the art class project became unbalanced.
It tilted a little. Then it tilted a lot.
Then it tipped entirely, knocking all the art supplies off-kilter as well.
"He just keeps at it," Mayor Wise explained to the governor.

"I've got it!" said Governor Bright.
"Obviously, they need . . ."

"... a louder bell."

First thing Thursday, the percussion-bomb bell was replaced by an avalanche-inducing contraption flown in from the Alps.

BLAAAAAAAAAAAAAARR

RRRRRRMMMMMMM!

It blasted like a ton of air horns getting smashed by a freight train.

The sound blew the ink off every whiteboard, and half the whiteboards off the walls, and a few walls out of place entirely.

But Henry did not stop his reading.
He decided to just stay put.

With the best player missing from PE, lots of balls rolled out of the gym . . .

. . . down the hall . . .

. . . and into the street . . .

It made *a little* extra work for the crossing guard.

"He has to be stopped," Governor Bright explained to the senator.

"I've got it!" said Senator Brilliant. "Indisputably, they need . . ."

"... a louder bell."

The next morning, the
air-horn-freight-train bell gave way
to a mega-giga-decibel monstrosity
illegal in seventeen states.

BRONKITYBRONKITYBRONKITY- BRONKITYBRONKITY!

It was louder than the Daytona 500, a squadron of Blue
Angels, and an army of door-to-door jackhammer sellers.
  The vibrations jittered every stitch of clothes in one direction.
They juttered every pair of shoes in the other.
They flung every backpack willy-nilly.

But Henry did not stop his reading.
He decided to just stay put.

Mayor Wise, Governor Bright, and Senator Brilliant considered what to do next.

"Hold on," said Ms. Sabio. "What if a *bigger* bell isn't the answer? What if we need something *simple*?"

Early the next day . . .

DING!
DING!

"But they aren't—"

"Shouldn't they be—"

"Why aren't they in school?"

"Because it's Saturday," said Henry.

"Oh," the mayor, the governor, and the senator replied. "So why are *we* just staying put?"

And they each made the most of their day, until long past the last bell.

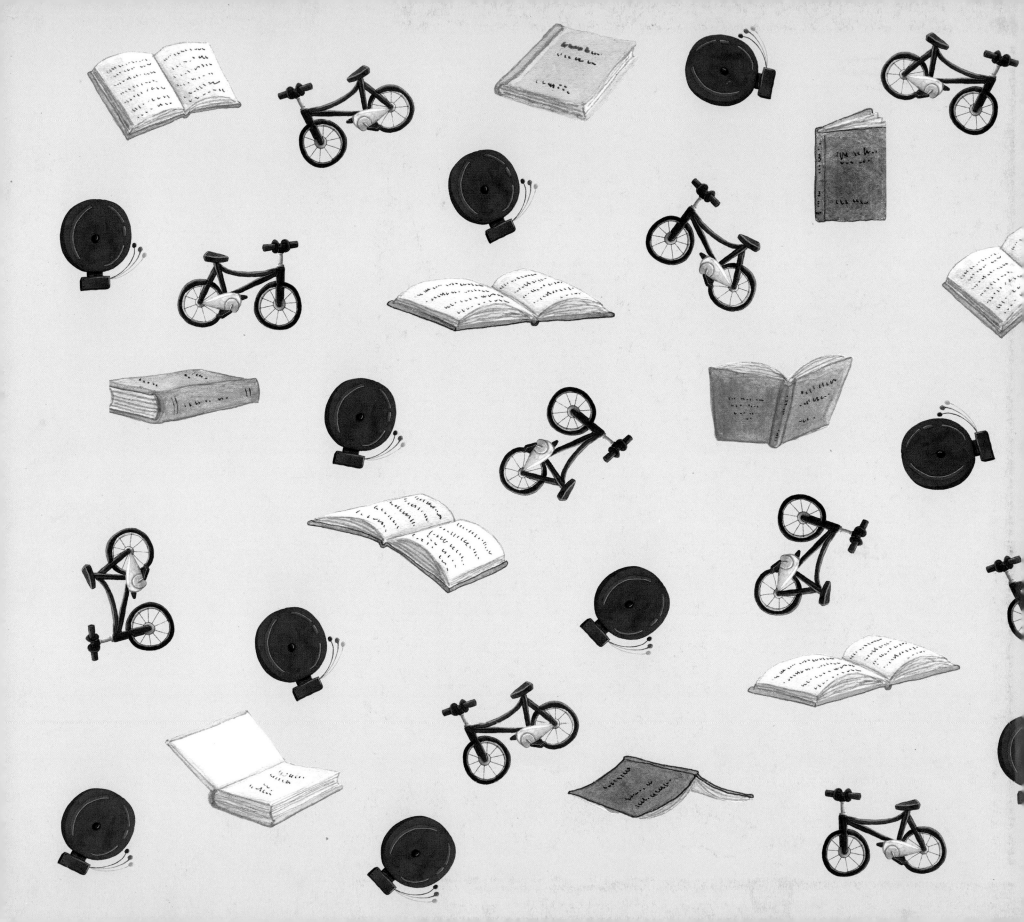